THIS BOOK

BELONGS TO:

. . . .

. . . .

Cecily Parsley's Nursery Rhymes

CECILY PARSLEY'S
NURSERY RHYMES

BY

BEATRIX POTTER

A PETER RABBIT™

110th Anniversary Edition

FREDERICK WARNE

FOR
LITTLE PETER
IN
NEW ZEALAND

FREDERICK WARNE

Published by the Penguin Group
Penguin Books Ltd., 80 Strand, London WC2R 0RL, England
Penguin Group (USA) Inc., 375 Hudson Street, New York, New York 10014, USA
Penguin Group (Australia), 250 Camberwell Road, Camberwell,
Victoria 3124, Australia (a division of Pearson Australia Group Pty. Ltd.)
Penguin Group (Canada), 90 Eglinton Avenue East, Suite 700, Toronto,
Ontario M4P 2Y3, Canada (a division of Pearson Penguin Canada Inc.)
Penguin Books India Pvt. Ltd., 11 Community Centre, Panchsheel Park, New Delhi—110 017, India
Penguin Group (NZ), 67 Apollo Drive, Rosedale, Auckland 0632,
New Zealand (a division of Pearson New Zealand Ltd.)
Penguin Books (South Africa) (Pty.) Ltd, 24 Sturdee Avenue, Rosebank, Johannesburg 2196, South Africa

Penguin Books Ltd., Registered Offices: 80 Strand, London WC2R 0RL, England

Website: www.peterrabbit.com

First published by Frederick Warne in 1922
First published with reset text and new reproductions
of Beatrix Potter's illustrations in 2002
This edition published in 2011

003 - 10 9 8 7 6 5 4 3

New reproductions copyright © Frederick Warne & Co., 2002
Original copyright in text and illustrations © Frederick Warne & Co., 1922
Frederick Warne & Co. is the owner of all rights, copyrights and trademarks
in the Beatrix Potter character names and illustrations.

Colour reproduction by
EAE Creative Colour Ltd, Norwich
Printed and bound in China

PUBLISHER'S NOTE

Cecily Parsley was Beatrix Potter's second book of nursery rhymes, but unlike Appley Dapply, it consisted not of original verse but mostly of traditional rhymes accompanied by Beatrix's illustrations.

In common with the earlier book, the drawings are a mixture of styles taken from different points in the artist's career.

Publishers Frederick Warne & Co. had initially hoped for another tale, but on receipt of Cecily Parsley decided to publish the book of rhymes for Christmas 1922.

CECILY PARSLEY
lived in a pen,
And brewed good ale
for gentlemen;

GENTLEMEN
came every day,
Till Cecily Parsley
ran away.

9

GOOSEY, GOOSEY, GANDER,
    Whither will you wander?
Upstairs and downstairs,
    And in my lady's chamber!

THIS pig went to market;
This pig stayed at home;

THIS pig had a bit of meat;

AND this pig had none;

This little pig cried
Wee! wee! wee!
I can't find my way home.

Pussy-cat sits by the fire;
        How should she be fair?
In walks the little dog,
        Says "Pussy! are you there?"

"How do you do, Mistress Pussy?
     Mistress Pussy, how do you do?"
"I thank you kindly, little dog,
     I fare as well as you!"

THREE blind mice, three blind mice,
See how they run!
They all run after the farmer's wife,
And she cut off their tails
with a carving knife,
Did ever you see such a thing
in your life
As three blind mice!

Bow, wow, wow!
    Whose dog art thou?
  "I'm little Tom Tinker's dog,
    Bow, wow, wow!"

We have a little garden,
  A garden of our own,
And every day we water there
  The seeds that we have sown.

WE love our little garden,
   And tend it with such care,
You will not find a faded leaf
   Or blighted blossom there.

Ninny Nanny Netticoat,
    In a white petticoat,
        With a red nose —
    The longer she stands,
        The shorter she grows.

THE END